THIS WALKER BOOK BELONGS TO:

_____

_____

_____

_____

For my illustrator friends
Elizabeth, Catherine, Rachel,
Paddy, Eliza and Fiona

First published 1986 by
Walker Books Ltd
87 Vauxhall Walk
London SE11 5HJ

This edition published 1988
Reprinted 1989

Printed in Italy by Grafedit S.p.A.

British Library Cataloguing in Publication Data
Daly, Niki
Just like Archie. — (Storytime).
I. Title   II. Series
823[J]   PZ7
ISBN 0-7445-0981-5

JUST LIKE
ARCHIE

Niki Daly

WALKER BOOKS
LONDON

Tom found a snail in
the garden.

'What have you got there?'
Mum asked.

'It's Archie,' Tom said.

'He's my pet.'

Mum frowned and said, 'I don't
think snails make good pets.'
Tom put Archie into a jam jar.
'I think he might like some
fresh leaves,' Mum said.

Tom ran back into the garden
to collect leaves.
While Tom was gone, Archie
crawled out of the jam jar
and went for a walk.

He crawled around a corner and
through a tunnel…

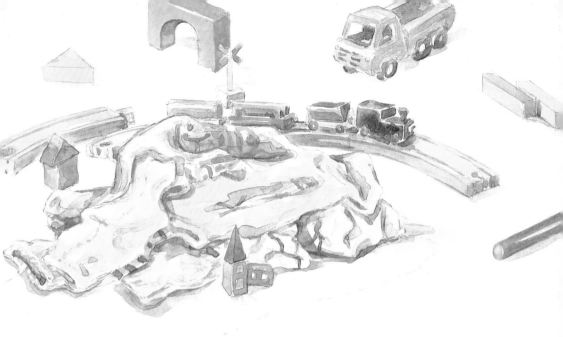

over a mountain…

and into Tom's sneaker.

When Tom came in, he found
the jar empty.
'Where's Archie?' Tom asked.

'I told you snails don't make
good pets,' Mum said.
But she helped him look anyway.

They looked everywhere but
they couldn't find Archie.

Then Tom saw a silvery trail
going around a corner, through
a tunnel, over a mountain…
and into his sneaker.
'Here he is!' Tom shouted.

Tom decided to put Archie back
in the garden. It made him feel
a little sad.

Mum said, 'Would you like a real
pet, Tom?'
'Yes,' said Tom. 'Someone like Archie.'
So Mum and Dad bought Tom a little
white mouse.
Tom called him Archie because…

he liked going for walks around
the corner, through a tunnel, over
a mountain…

and into Tom's sneaker.

Just like Archie!

MORE WALKER PAPERBACKS

BABIES' FIRST BOOKS

Marie Wabbes
Little Rabbit
LITTLE RABBIT'S GARDEN
GOOD NIGHT, LITTLE RABBIT

PICTURE BOOKS
For The Very Young

Helen Oxenbury
Pippo
No. 1 TOM & PIPPO READ A STORY
No. 2 TOM & PIPPO MAKE A MESS
No. 3 TOM & PIPPO GO FOR A WALK
No. 4 TOM & PIPPO AND THE
WASHING MACHINE
No. 5 TOM & PIPPO GO SHOPPING
No. 6 TOM & PIPPO'S DAY
No. 7 TOM & PIPPO IN THE GARDEN
No. 8 TOM & PIPPO SEE THE MOON

LEARNING FOR FUN
The Pre-School Years

Shirley Hughes
Nursery Collection
NOISY
COLOURS
BATHWATER'S HOT
ALL SHAPES AND SIZES
TWO SHOES, NEW SHOES
WHEN WE WENT TO THE PARK

John Burningham
Concept Books
COLOURS   ALPHABET
OPPOSITES   NUMBERS

Philippe Dupasquier
Busy Places
THE GARAGE   THE AIRPORT
THE BUILDING SITE
THE FACTORY   THE HARBOUR
THE RAILWAY STATION

Tony Wells   Puzzle Books
PUZZLE DOUBLES
ALLSORTS